FAIRY TALES

RETOLD BY JAMES RIORDAN
ILLUSTRATED BY HILDA OFFEN

FAIRY TALES

RETOLD BY JAMES RIORDAN
ILLUSTRATED BY HILDA OFFEN

Cathay Books

First published in 1987 by
Octopus Books Limited,
Michelin House,
81 Fulham Road,
London SW3 6RB.
Reprinted 1988, 1990
© Copyright Octopus Books Limited 1987
ISBN 0 8081 6310 8
Printed and bound in Hong Kong

Contents

GOLDILOCKS AND THE THREE BEARS

Once upon a time there were three bears: a great big Father Bear, a middle-sized Mother Bear, and a little Baby Bear. They all lived together in a cottage in the woods.

Early one morning, they made porridge for breakfast and filled three bowls with it. There was a great big bowl for Father Bear, a middle-sized bowl for Mother Bear, and a teeny-weeny bowl for Baby Bear. But the porridge was too hot to eat straight away and, since they did not want to burn their mouths, the three bears went for a walk in the woods while their porridge cooled.

On the very edge of the woods lived a little girl with her mother and father. She had lovely golden curls, and everybody called her Goldilocks. That day she went for a walk in the woods and even though her mother had warned her not to go too far, she followed a trail of flowers farther and farther into the woods. She listened to the birds singing and looked at the pretty flowers and wandered on until she was quite lost.

After a while she came to a wooden house in the middle of the woods. It was the cottage where the three bears lived.

'Oh, what a lovely house,' said Goldilocks. 'I wonder if there's anyone in.' She knocked at the door: toc-toc-toc. As there was no answer she knocked again, and again. Then she peeped through the keyhole; but there was no one at home.

'I'll just look inside,' thought Goldilocks. 'The door is not locked.' So she lifted the latch, opened the door and walked in. She found herself inside a neat and tidy little house.

The first things she saw as she looked around were three chairs. Feeling tired and being a curious little girl, she climbed on to Father Bear's great big chair. 'Oh dear, this chair's much too hard,' she said. So she went over to the second chair.

When she sat in Mother Bear's chair, she cried, 'Oh dear, this chair's too soft.' So she went over to the third chair.

When she sat down on Baby Bear's little chair, she said, 'Ah, this chair's not too hard and not too soft. It is just right.'

But Goldilocks was too heavy for the little chair and as she rocked back on its legs, she heard a crack. One of its legs broke and she fell on to the floor with a bump.

She picked herself up and dusted herself off. Then she noticed the three bowls of porridge. Steam was rising from them and they smelt delicious. Since she had had no breakfast, the smell of porridge made her very hungry.

'I'll just taste a little from each bowl,' she thought to herself. 'That way no one will notice that some has gone.' So she picked up a spoon and tried the porridge in Father Bear's great big bowl. 'Ouch, this is too hot,' she cried.

Next she dipped a spoon into Mother Bear's middle-sized bowl and tried the porridge there. 'Ugh, this porridge is too cold,' she said.

Then she tried the porridge in Baby Bear's teeny-weeny bowl. 'Ooh, this is not too hot and not too cold. It's just right.'

She liked it so much she ate it all up.

When she had eaten the porridge she decided to take a further look about the house. So she climbed the stairs to see what she could find in the bedroom.

There were three beds standing in a row. There was Father Bear's great big bed, Mother Bear's middle-sized bed and Baby Bear's teeny-weeny bed.

Feeling tired after her long walk and after eating porridge, Goldilocks thought she would take a rest on a bed. First she lay down on the great big bed. 'Oh dear,' she cried, 'this bed's much too hard.'

Next she tried the middle-sized bed, but found that not to her liking either. 'Oh dear,' she said, 'this one's too lumpy.'

Last of all she tried the teeny-weeny bed. 'Ah, this one's not too hard and not too lumpy. It's just right.'

She felt so snug and cosy that in no time at all she fell fast asleep with her head on Baby Bear's little pillow.

Presently, the three bears returned from their walk and were surprised to find the front door open. As he entered the house and looked around, Father Bear noticed that his chair was out of place. 'Somebody's been sitting on my chair,' he said in his great big voice.

Mother Bear noticed that her cushion was rumpled. 'Someone's been sitting on my chair,' she said in her middle-sized voice.

Then Baby Bear took a look at his chair. 'Someone's been sitting on my chair and broken the leg right off,' he cried in his teeny-weeny voice. And he began to cry.

As the three bears looked about them, they noticed something wrong with the bowls of porridge on the table. First Father Bear saw that his spoon was in the wrong place. 'Someone's been eating my porridge,' he said in his great big voice.

Then Mother Bear saw her spoon in her porridge. 'Someone's been eating my porridge,' she said in her middle-sized voice.

When Baby Bear looked into his bowl, he began to wail in his teeny-weeny voice, 'Someone's been eating my porridge and eaten it all up.' And he started to cry once more.

The bears searched all through the house and finally climbed the stairs to see if their visitor was in the bedroom. As soon as they entered the room Father Bear noticed that his blanket was not straight. 'Someone's been sleeping in my bed,' he said in his great big voice.

Then Mother Bear saw that her pillow was crumpled. 'Someone's been sleeping in my bed,' she said in her middle-sized voice.

When Baby Bear looked at his bed he saw Goldilocks fast asleep there. He was so surprised that he let out a shrill cry and said in his teeny-weeny voice, 'Someone's been sleeping in my bed and here she still is!'

Now, when Father Bear was speaking, his voice boomed out like thunder. Yet Goldilocks did not wake up. When Mother Bear was speaking, her middle-sized voice sounded like the wind in the trees. Yet still Goldilocks did not wake up. But when Baby Bear cried in his teeny-weeny voice Goldilocks woke up and sat up in bed with a start, rubbing her eyes. How scared she was to see the three bears staring down at her.

Before the bears could move, Goldilocks was out of bed and down the stairs, out of the door and through the trees. She did not stop running until she reached her own house. Never was she more pleased to see her mother.

Breathlessly she told her story: how she was lost, found the little house, broke the little chair, ate the porridge and slept in Baby Bear's bed. But she learned her lesson, and she never went off alone into the woods again.

LITTLE RED RIDING HOOD

Once upon a time there lived a little girl who was loved by all who knew her. Her grandmother made her a red hood like the ones fine ladies used to wear when out riding, and she wore it with her velvet cloak wherever she went. People soon began to call her Little Red Riding Hood.

One day, her grandmother was not well so her mother baked some cakes and told Little Red Riding Hood to take them with a pot of butter and see how she was. Now her grandmother lived in a village on the other side of the wood, so Little Red Riding Hood had to walk through the wood when she went to visit her. Her mother always warned her before she set off not to talk to any strangers on the way to her grandmother.

That morning, Little Red Riding Hood put the cakes and butter in her basket and, wearing her red hood and cloak, set off down the path.

Not long after she entered the wood she met a wicked wolf. The wolf wanted to eat her there and then, but he dared not because there were some woodcutters nearby. Instead, he greeted her politely, saying, 'Good morning to you, Little Red Riding Hood. Where are you going?'

Forgetting her mother's warning, the little girl stopped and said, 'I'm going to Grandmother's.'

'And what have you in your basket?' asked the wolf.

'Some cakes and a little pot of butter. They're for Grandmother because she's not well.'

'Oh I am sorry,' said the wolf. 'Does she live far away?'

'She lives through the wood, beyond the mill, at the first house in the village.'

'I see,' said the wolf. 'Then I'll go to see her too. I'll take this path, you take that, and we'll see who gets there first.'

Little Red Riding Hood continued on her way, picking bluebells and primroses, making little daisy chains and chasing butterflies as she went. But the big bad wolf took a short cut and in no time at all he arrived at Grandmother's cottage.

He knocked hard on the door: rat-tat-tat-tat.

'Who's there?' came a frail voice from inside.

'It's me, Little Red Riding Hood,' said the wolf in a high voice. 'I've brought you some cakes and a little pot of butter.'

'Lift the latch and come in,' said Grandmother from her bed.

So the wolf lifted the latch, opened the door and went in. Without more ado he went up to the bed and swallowed the old woman in a single gulp. He was very hungry, not having eaten for three whole days.

Then he put on her nightdress, spectacles and nightcap, got into bed and lay waiting for Little Red Riding Hood to arrive.

At last she came to the cottage and knocked at the door: rat-tat-tat-tat.

'Who's there?' said the wolf.

Hearing the wolf's gruff voice, the little girl was at first afraid. Then, remembering Grandmother had a cold, she replied, 'It's me, your granddaughter, Little Red Riding Hood. I've brought you some of Mother's cakes and a little pot of butter.'

Doing his best to hide his gruff voice, the wolf called, 'Lift the latch and open the door, my dear.'

19

So Little Riding Hood lifted the latch, opened the door and went in.

The wolf quickly pulled the bedclothes up to his nose, tucked his big ears under the nightcap and peered over the top of Grandmother's spectacles. Then he said in a muffled voice, 'Put the cakes and pot of butter on the stool and come and sit on the bed.'

Little Red Riding Hood did as she was told, but she thought her grandmother looked rather strange, especially as two big ears were now poking out from under the nightcap.

'Oh Grandmother,' said Red Riding Hood, 'what big ears you have.'

'All the better to hear you with, my dear,' said the wolf.

'Oh Grandmother, what big eyes you have.'

'All the better to see you with, my dear.'

Seeing the wolf's big hairy paws, the little girl said in a frightened voice, 'Oh Grandmother, what big hands you have.'

'All the better to hold you with, my dear.'

'Oh Grandmother, what big teeth you have.'

'All the better to eat you with, my dear.'

With that the wolf sprang out of bed and swallowed Little Red Riding Hood in one gulp. He was so full now, that he lay down on the bed again to sleep and was soon snoring loudly.

Not long after, a woodcutter passed by the cottage and heard the terrible snores. 'That's strange,' he said to himself. 'I wonder if the old lady is all right.'

He opened the cottage door and went over to the bed. Imagine his surprise when instead of finding the old lady he found the wolf fast asleep. Realizing that the beast must have eaten the old woman, he took his knife and cut open the wolf's belly for he hoped that the wolf had eaten her whole.

Out jumped Little Red Riding Hood, alive and well. 'Oh how dark it was inside the wolf,' she said.

Next Grandmother scrambled out, feeling very shocked. But she ate her cakes and pot of butter and soon felt better. As for Little Red Riding Hood, she ran home to her mother and promised never again to talk to strangers in the wood.

HANSEL AND GRETEL

Once upon a time there was a woodcutter and his wife who lived in a cottage at the edge of the wood. One day, when times were hard, they realized that they could no longer feed their two children, Hansel and Gretel. So they made up their minds to take them to the depths of the forest and leave them there.

'The children will stand as much chance on their own,' the woodcutter said, 'as they will at home with no food.'

At daybreak, therefore, the parents took Hansel and Gretel far into the forest and, telling them to wait in a glade while they gathered brushwood, the two trudged sadly home.

By evening, Hansel and Gretel were very frightened and began to cry. They called for their mother and father but no one came. Soon it was pitch dark and they could barely see a hand before their face. They sank down beneath a giant oak tree and, clasped in each other's arms, they lay trembling upon the mossy soil. As they were lying there the Sandman came and gently sprinkled his magic dust in their eyes to make them sleep, and in a few moments they were both fast asleep.

At sunrise next day they awoke and began to wander through the trees, hungry and scared. On and on they went until, towards midday, they spotted a strange little bird with feathers as white as snow. It was sitting on a branch and singing so sweetly that they stood still and listened to it. When it had finished, it flapped its wings and flew off in front of them, leading them on until they came to a cottage in the centre of a sunlit glade. The little white bird settled upon the cottage roof.

As the children drew near, they saw that the house was built of cakes and gingerbread, the windows were made of barley sugar, and the roof — well it was made of the most delicious cakes you could imagine.

To one side of the house stood a big oven, to the other stood a wooden cage. And around it all was a fence of gingerbread cut into figures of little children. In truth, though the children did not know it, this was the dwelling of a wicked witch, and the figures in the fence were those poor children she had baked into gingerbread.

Hansel and Gretel could not believe their eyes. Just the sight of all the food made their mouths water, and in next to no time they were breaking off pieces of cake and barley sugar from the walls and windows. But in the middle of their munching, a weedy little voice came from inside the house:

> '*Nibble, nibble, mousey,*
> *Who's nibbling at my housey?'*

And the children answered back,

> '*The wind, the wind,*
> *The wandering wind.'*

They continued their nibbling and were so busy that neither of them noticed the wicked witch creep out of her house. She sniffed

There now began a terrifying time for the poor children. The best food was cooked for Hansel, but Gretel had nothing but frogs and snails. Each morning the horrible old crone would go to the cage and call, 'Hansel, Hansel, poke your finger through the bars for me to feel how fat you are.'

But Hansel would push a twig through the bars of his cage, and the short-sighted witch would take it for his finger. How puzzled she was that he never seemed to grow any plumper. No matter how much food she fed him, he seemed to stay as skinny as a broomstick.

After a few weeks the witch lost patience. She screeched at Gretel, 'I'm fed up with waiting. Light a fire in the yard, fill the pot with water and set it on to boil. I'm going to boil that brat, skinny or fat.'

How Gretel cried, but there was nothing for it: she had to do as she was told. The wicked witch kneaded some dough and stoked up the oven and soon, large red flames were pouring out.

'Now peep inside the oven and see if it is hot enough for baking,' the witch said to Gretel. Of course, she was intending to push the girl into the oven and bake her alive so she could eat two children: one boiled, one baked.

But Gretel saw through her plan. Pretending to be stupid, she whimpered, 'But Granny, I don't know how. Please show me what to do.'

'Stupid girl,' cried the witch angrily. 'Look, see, watch . . .'
Thereupon, she bent forward towards the open oven and began

to feel the heat with her skinny hands. In an instant, Gretel gave her a hard push so that she tumbled head first, right into the red-hot oven! Then the girl banged shut the iron door and dropped the bar. Whoosh! Bang! Aiyeee! The witch was burnt to a frazzle.

Without more ado, Gretel ran to her brother's cage and flung the door wide open. The two children hugged and kissed and danced with happiness.

'The wicked witch is dead! Hooray, we're free,' they sang.

Suddenly, there came a great rumbling like distant thunder, and, as the children stared, the oven exploded leaving a column of black smoke and a trail of blue, foul-smelling gas. All that remained of the oven was a huge loaf of gingerbread.

Then something else happened. The gingerbread figures in the fence turned into real, live girls and boys. When the witch died, the spell on them was broken but they stood motionless, unable to see, or hear, or speak. Quickly, Gretel fetched the juniper bough and uttered the magic words she had heard. The boys and girls opened their eyes, stretched their arms and smiled warm, grateful smiles.

As the children were coming to life, Hansel and Gretel went into the witch's house and found in every corner great chests of pearls and gold and precious stones. They filled some sacks with the treasure, then set off to find their home.

They had not gone far, when they came upon the strange white bird again. This time, it guided them all the way back to their cottage. There the children emptied their sacks of treasure upon the floor. How happy everyone was. All their troubles were over and they never lacked for food again.

JACK AND THE BEANSTALK

Once upon a time there was a widow with an only son called Jack. She tended to spoil the lad and he grew up lazy and disobedient. One by one she sold all her possessions so that her son could be happy, until all she had left was a cow. The widow was sorry to part with the cow, but there was nothing for it. So, one morning, she told her son to take it to market.

Off went Jack to market with the cow but he had not gone far when he met a strange old man.

'Where are you driving that cow?' the stranger asked.

'I'm taking her to market,' Jack replied.

At that, the stranger took off his hat and shook it. Jack stared when he saw it was full of beans of every colour. Seeing his interest in the beans, the strange old man offered all the beans in his hat in exchange for the cow. The silly boy could not resist what seemed to him a bargain. The deal was struck, the cow and beans handed over, and Jack hurried home to tell his mother the good news.

When the poor woman saw the beans, she lost all patience. 'What? You stupid boy. You have sold our cow for these miserable beans! Give them to me.'

As Jack put out his hand with the beans, his mother hit it hard, knocking the beans in all directions about the garden. Then she packed him off to bed without his supper. Poor Jack, sad and sorry for himself, made his way upstairs to his little room, and soon fell asleep.

Early next morning, when he awoke, he saw an odd shadow on his bed. It was coming from something tall outside his window. Running downstairs to the garden, he soon discovered what it was. Some of the beans had taken root and sprung up, and they were twisting and turning into a giant beanstalk.

It was so tall that as Jack gazed up he could not see the top; it vanished into the clouds. Wanting to know what was up there, he put his foot on the beanstalk and finding it firm, he began to climb: up and up and up.

After some time, he reached the top of the beanstalk and was surprised to find himself in a strange land. It was like a desert: empty and deserted, with no trees or shrubs or houses. There were no people or animals, just rough stone and rocks scattered about. He started to walk, and at sunset he came to a big castle. At the door stood a woman as tall as a house.

'Good evening,' said Jack politely. 'Could you give me a bit of bread and a night's lodging?'

'What are you doing here?' she answered. 'Don't you know that my husband is a giant who eats human flesh? He'll have you on toast for supper if he catches you.'

Poor Jack shivered and shook, wishing he was back home with his mother. But he was very hungry and he begged the woman for food. She was a kind soul, and felt sorry for Jack, so she took him in and gave him a great hunk of bread and cheese, as well as a jug of milk. He had almost finished eating when, all at once, the castle began to shake and he heard, thump, thump, thump, thump. It was the giant coming.

'Quick,' said the woman, 'hide in the oven.'

Quick as a flash, Jack jumped into the giant oven and peeped out into the kitchen. He saw the giant enter and heard him roar like thunder:

'Fee, fi, fo, fum,
I smell the blood of an Englishman.'

'Oh, no, my dear,' said his wife. 'It's only the prisoners in the dungeon.'

The giant seemed satisfied and sat down to supper. After he had eaten he said to his wife, 'Bring me the goose that lays the golden eggs.'

33

The woman brought in a goose, and Jack was surprised to see that every time the giant said 'Lay', the goose laid an egg of shining gold. At length the giant grew tired and fell asleep, and his snoring was like the boom-boom-booming of a cannon.

After a while, Jack crept out of the oven, snatched up the golden goose and ran off with it. He reached the beanstalk and scrambled down it as fast as he could.

'Now, Mother,' said Jack, 'I've brought you a present that will make us rich for the rest of our days.' With that he put the goose upon the table and told it to lay eggs.

Immediately, the goose produced as many golden eggs as they desired; Jack sold the eggs and he and his mother became rich beyond their wildest dreams.

Jack, however, was not content. He longed to climb the beanstalk and pay the giant another visit. So, despite his mother's warnings, he got up early one morning and climbed the beanstalk again: up and up and up, through the clouds.

Making his way to the castle, he found the woman as tall as a house standing at the door, just as before.

'Hello,' said Jack politely. 'Could you give me a bit of bread and a night's lodging? I'm so tired and hungry.'

'Just a minute, aren't you the lad that came here before?' said the woman. 'He asked for food and bed and then stole one of my husband's treasures. My husband has never forgiven me.'

'Oh no,' said Jack. 'It wasn't me. I'd never do a thing like that. Please let me in.'

'Well, all right,' said the woman at last and she gave him a big hunk of bread and cheese, and giant pickles too. This time he had a jug of beer to wash it down. But scarcely had he eaten, than the castle began to shake and he heard, thump, thump, thump, thump. It was the giant coming.

Jack almost froze in terror remembering the horrible sight of the huge giant.

'Quick,' said the great big woman, 'hide in the broom cupboard.'

As Jack hid he heard the giant roar:

  'Fee, fi, fo, fum,
  I smell the blood of an Englishman.'

'Oh no, my dear,' said his wife. 'It's only the crows on the roof who've brought some meat.'

The giant seemed content. He ate his supper then called out, 'Fetch my bags of gold and silver. I wish to count my money.'

His wife soon appeared, staggering under the weight of the two money bags. Jack watched from his hiding place as the giant poured the glittering golden sovereigns and silver shillings upon the table. He counted and recounted the coins until he fell asleep, snoring like the roar of the raging sea as it crashes upon the shore.

Then Jack seized his chance. He tiptoed from the broom cupboard, picked up both bags and somehow managed to carry them to the beanstalk and down to the ground.

With their new-found wealth Jack and his mother repaired and refurnished their cottage and lived in comfort for a whole year, and

then a second year. As time went by, however, Jack wished to try his luck one last time in the giant's castle.

So one morning, early, before his mother was up, he climbed the beanstalk and reached the giant's castle, where he found the woman as tall as a house standing at the door.

All went as before until the giant returned. Thump, thump, thump, thump. This time Jack hid in the wash-tub.

As soon as the giant entered, he roared out:

'Fee, fi, fo, fum,
I smell the blood of an Englishman.'

His wife tried to reassure him, but this time the giant was not convinced. He began to search high and low; and even put his hand on the wash-tub. Poor Jack almost jumped out of his skin.

At last the giant gave up and sat down to supper. When he had finished, he shouted out, 'Wife, fetch my golden harp.'

As Jack peeped out of the copper wash-tub, he saw the most beautiful golden harp. The moment the giant said 'Play', it played of its own accord such lovely music. It soon lulled the giant into a sound sleep, and he began to snore in tune with the music.

That was Jack's chance. He climbed out of the tub, seized the golden harp and started to run off with it. Yet the moment he picked it up, the harp cried out loudly, 'Master, Master, Master!'

At once the giant awoke and stumbled after Jack. He had had so much to drink that he was unsteady on his feet and kept running round in circles. But Jack made for the beanstalk and clambered down. As soon as he could see the bottom of the beanstalk he cried out, 'Mother, Mother, quick, fetch an axe.'

By the time he reached the ground, his mother was ready with the axe. It was just as well, for the giant was climbing down the beanstalk and it was shaking and swaying under his weight. Soon his legs could be seen coming through the clouds.

Jack swung the axe and cut right through the beanstalk. It toppled over with a crash and the giant came tumbling with it, the mighty fall killing him instantly.

Jack was kind and loving to his mother from then on, and they both lived in peace and happiness for the rest of their days. And all the time, Jack of course took great care of the goose that lays the golden eggs, the bags of silver and gold, and the golden harp.

RUMPELSTILTSKIN

Once upon a time there was a miller who was very poor. His one treasure was his only daughter of whom he was very proud.

One day, letting his tongue run away with him, he boasted to the king, 'I've a daughter who can spin straw into gold.'

'If your daughter is as clever as you say,' said the king, 'bring her here and we'll see if it is so.'

So the miller went home and told his daughter to prepare herself. She put on her best dress, brushed her hair and went before the king. The king at once led her to a room full of straw, with a spinning wheel and stool in one corner.

'Now set to work,' he said, 'and spin this straw into gold. If the work is not done by morning you will die.' With that he went off, locking the door behind him.

39

What was the miller's daughter to do? How could anyone spin straw into gold? Sitting on the stool, she began to cry.

All of a sudden, she heard a strange noise from behind the door and it opened of its own accord, just wide enough to let in an ugly little man.

'Good evening, Missus,' he said. 'Why are you crying?'

'I have to spin straw into gold,' she said, 'and I don't know how to do it. If I don't succeed, I shall be killed at dawn.'

'What will you give me if I do it for you?' asked the little man.

'Would you take my necklace?'

'Done,' he said. Then he took the necklace, sat down before the spinning wheel and set to work. Whirr, whirr, whirr. Blur, blur, blur. The miller's daughter could not see straw for gold. All night long the little man worked and by daybreak all the straw was spun into purest gold. Then he disappeared.

Soon after daybreak the king came back. How surprised he was
to see the gold. But it only made him greedy for more, so he led the
miller's daughter to an even bigger room full of straw.

'Now set to work,' he said, 'and spin this straw into gold. You
have till morning.' Off he went, locking the door behind him.

Once more the poor girl sat upon the stool and began to cry.
But then she heard the same scratching noise and saw the door open
just wide enough to let in the odd little man.

'Good morrow, Missus,' he said. 'What is wrong this time?'

'Now I have to spin even more straw into gold,' she said. 'If I
don't, I'm to die at dawn.'

'What will you give me if I do it for you?'

'Will you take my ring?'

'That I will,' he said. So he took the ring, sat himself down
before the spinning wheel and set to work. Whirr, whirr, whirr.
Blur, blur, blur. The miller's daughter could not see straw for gold.

All day and night the little man worked and by dawn all the straw was spun into gold. Then he vanished in a puff of smoke.

When the king unlocked the door in the morning he rubbed his hands with glee at the sight of all the gold. But still he was not satisfied. He had the miller's daughter taken into another room, even bigger than the second. It too was stacked with straw from floor to rafters.

'Now set to work,' he said, 'and spin this straw into gold by dawn. If you succeed, I'll marry you.' With that he locked the door, leaving her alone.

As soon as he was gone, the ugly little fellow appeared, saying, 'What will you give me if I do the work for you?'

'I've nothing more to give,' the girl said sadly.

'Then promise me your first child when you are queen.'

The girl did not like that idea at all, but what could she do? In any case, she might never have a child, so she she gave her word.

Then the strange little man sat down before the wheel and set to work. Whirr, whirr, whirr. Blur, blur, blur. The miller's daughter could not see straw for gold. Eventually the straw was spun into gold and the ugly man disappeared.

The next morning when the king came in, he found all as he had asked. So he married the miller's daughter there and then, making her his queen.

43

A year passed, and the young queen had a baby boy, as fair a child as ever was seen. By then, all thought of the little man had left her head, until all of a sudden there he was before her, demanding his due.

The queen was horrified. She cried and clutched the baby tightly to her breast. In the end, moved by her pleas and tears, the little man told her, 'I'll give you three days to guess my name. If you do, you may keep your child.'

All night long the queen thought of every name she had ever heard, and next morning, when the man appeared, she went right through the ABC, 'Amadeus, Balthazar, Caspar . . .'

At each name he shook his head and grinned from ear to ear. 'Tisn't me,' he said. At last he disappeared.

On the second day he returned. 'What's my name?' he asked. She tried all the oddest names she knew but to each he shook

his head and grinned from ear to ear. 'Tisn't me,' he said and finally
he disappeared.

Next morning the queen sent out messengers far and wide to
collect all the names they could find. But it seemed she had already
spoken all the names, for they did not find a single new one. One
messenger, however, said he had seen a strange sight. 'I saw a little
house in a valley; and in front of the house was a fire round which
danced the strangest little man I've ever seen. As he hopped up and
down he sang this song:

"*Today I bake, tomorrow I brew,*
Then, dear prince, I come for you.
None can guess, none can claim
That Rumpelstiltskin is my name."'

The queen jumped for joy
when the messenger finished the
song, but when the little man
came that night, his eyes shining
like red-hot coals, she at first
pretended not to know his name.

'What's my name? What's
my name?' he sang, dancing up
and down, and he grinned from
ear to ear, rubbing his hands in glee.

'It's Robin.'

'Tisn't.'

'It's Jack.'

'Tisn't.

'Then Rumpelstiltskin is your name.'

When the little man heard that he flew into a terrible rage.
'The devil must have told you!' he shrieked, and he stamped his feet
so hard that he disappeared right through the floor and was never
seen again.

THE THREE BILLY GOATS GRUFF

Once upon a time there were three billy goats Gruff. They lived in a field, at the bottom of a hill, and on the hill was juicy green grass. How they longed to go up the hillside, to eat the grass and grow fat.

The only trouble was, that on the way they had to cross a bridge over a stream. And under the bridge lived a wicked troll, with eyes as big as saucers and a nose as long as a broomstick.

One day, when there was no more grass in their field, the three billy goats Gruff decided to go to the hillside to eat the grass there. So off they went, one at a time, towards the bridge.

First to reach the bridge was the youngest billy goat Gruff. His feet went trip-trap, trip-trap on to the bridge.

47

'Who's that trip-trapping over my bridge?' roared the troll from under the bridge.

'It's only me, little billy goat Gruff,' he said in a tiny voice. 'I'm going to the hillside to eat grass.'

'Oh no you're not. I'm going to come up and eat you,' said the troll.

'Oh no, please don't eat me. I'm too little. Wait for middle billy goat Gruff; he's much bigger than me.'

'Oh, all right,' grumbled the troll. 'Go on your way.'

So the youngest billy goat Gruff ran, trip-trap, trip-trap over the bridge and on to the hillside.

Soon after, middle billy goat Gruff came to the bridge. His feet went TRIP-TRAP, TRIP-TRAP on to the bridge.

'Who's that trip-trapping over my bridge?' roared the troll from under the bridge.

'It's only me, middle billy goat Gruff,' he said in a middle-sized voice. 'I'm going to the hillside to eat grass.'

'Oh no you're not,' said the troll. 'I'm going to come up and eat you.'

'Oh no, please don't eat me. I'm much too small. Wait for big billy goat Gruff; he's much bigger than me.'

'Oh, all right,' grumbled the troll. 'Be on your way.'

So the middle billy goat Gruff ran TRIP-TRAP, TRIP-TRAP over the bridge and on to the hillside.

Presently, along came big billy goat Gruff. His feet went TRIP-TRAP, TRIP-TRAP on to the bridge. Big billy goat Gruff was so heavy the bridge creaked and groaned beneath him.

'Who's that trip-trapping over my bridge,' roared the troll from under the bridge.

'It is me, big billy goat Gruff,' he said in a deep, deep voice. 'I'm going to the hillside to eat grass.'

'Oh no you're not,' roared the troll. 'I'm going to come up and eat you.'

'Come up and eat me! Come up and eat me!' shouted back big billy goat Gruff. 'Just you try. I have two sharp horns and I shall kill you first.'

When the ugly troll appeared on the bridge, big billy goat Gruff rushed at him with his long horns and tossed him into the stream. Then he crossed the bridge, heavy and slow, TRIP-TRAP, TRIP-TRAP, and went to join the other two billy goats Gruff on the hillside. Together, they ate the juicy green grass to their heart's content.

They grew so fat they could scarcely walk home again. And if the fat has not gone, they're just as fat still.

THE LITTLE GINGERBREAD MAN

Once upon a time there was a little old woman and a little old man. And they lived together in a little old house. They were very poor and could hardly buy enough to eat, but one day the little old woman said, 'Cheer up, old man. I'll make a little man out of gingerbread.'

'But we have no flour,' grumbled her husband.

'If I scratch around the loft I might find a few ears of corn,' she replied. 'Then I'll grind the corn into flour, make some dough, roll it out and cut it into the shape of a little man. I'll add currants for eyes, a nose and a mouth and some down the front for a jacket. When all's ready I'll pop it into the oven to bake, crisp and brown.'

Off she went and returned shortly with a few ears of corn. She ground the corn into flour, made some dough, rolled it out and cut it into shape. She added currants for eyes, a nose and a mouth and some down the front for a jacket. That done, she popped it into the oven to bake, crisp and brown.

After a time she opened the oven door and out hopped a little gingerbread man. Before she could catch him he hopped across the floor, straight out of the door, down the path and through the gate. As he ran along he sang out loud and clear,

'*Run, run, as fast as you can,*
You can't catch me, I'm the gingerbread man.'

Although the little old woman and the little old man ran after him, they could not catch him.

As he ran down the street he passed some children playing. When they saw the little gingerbread man, they called out, 'Yum, yum, yum, you look good enough to eat.'

But the little gingerbread man only laughed as he ran on, calling back,

'*Run, run, as fast as you can,*
You can't catch me, I'm the gingerbread man.'

Although the children ran after him, followed by the little old woman and the little old man, they could not catch him.

He ran on and on until he passed a cat. When it saw the little gingerbread man, it called out, 'Purr, purr, purr, you look good enough to eat.'

But the little gingerbread man only laughed and ran faster than ever, shouting back,

> '*Run, run, as fast as you can,*
> *You can't catch me, I'm the gingerbread man.*'

Although the cat ran after him, followed by the children, the little old woman and the little old man, it could not catch him.

On and on he ran till he passed a dog. The dog barked out, 'Woof, woof, woof, you look good enough to eat.'

But the little gingerbread man only laughed and ran on faster than ever, shouting back,

> '*Run, run, as fast as you can,*
> *You can't catch me, I'm the gingerbread man.*'

The dog ran hard behind, followed by the cat, the children, the little old woman and the little old man, but it could not catch him.

On and on ran the little gingerbread man until he reached a river. Now he had to stop for he did not know how to swim across. As he was standing there, a fox came along and said, 'Well, hello there, gingerbread man. Do you want to cross the river?'

'Yes, I do,' said the little gingerbread man.

'Then jump on my tail and I'll take you across.'

So the little gingerbread man hopped on to the fox's tail and the fox began to swim across the river.

When it was half-way over, the fox turned its head and said, 'You are heavy on my tail, move forward to my back.'

So the little gingerbread man moved forward on to the fox's back.

After a while the fox said, 'You're too heavy on my back, move forward to my neck.'

So the little gingerbread man sat forward upon the fox's neck, and the fox swam on.

Then the fox said, 'You're heavy on my neck, move forward to my nose.'

So the little gingerbread man sat astride the fox's nose.

With that the fox threw back its head. SNAP!

And that was the end of the gingerbread man.

SNOW WHITE

O nce, long ago, there lived a king and queen who had a beautiful daughter. Her skin was as white as snow, her lips were red as blood and her hair was black as ebony. She was called Snow White.

When Snow White was very young, the good queen died and the king married again. The new queen could not bear the thought that someone might be prettier than her. So, she would look into a magic mirror and say,

'Mirror, mirror on the wall,
Who is the fairest one of all?'

The mirror would reply,

'You, oh Queen, are the fairest in the land.'

And the queen was content for she knew the mirror always told the truth. But one day, the queen spoke to her mirror as usual,

'Mirror, mirror on the wall,
Who is the fairest one of all?'

And the mirror replied,

'You, oh Queen, are fair, 'tis true,
But Snow White is now fairer than you.'

The queen was furious. She summoned a huntsman and ordered him to kill Snow White. Obediently, he took Snow White deep into the forest where he took out his knife to kill her. Yet he could not do the foul deed and left her to fend for herself in the forest.

Snow White stumbled along until she came to a tiny house. Inside, a meal for seven was on the table. She was very hungry so she ate some food then lay on a bed and fell fast asleep.

That evening the masters of the house came home. They were seven dwarfs who spent their days digging for gold and diamonds in the mountains. When they saw Snow White they all agreed, 'What a beautiful girl,' and they did not disturb her.

In the morning when Snow White awoke, she told the kind dwarfs her story. They asked her to stay with them as long as she wished, and for a while she did.

One day, however, the wicked queen spoke to her mirror:
        'Mirror, mirror, on the wall,
        Who is the fairest one of all?'
And the mirror replied,
        'You, oh Queen, are fair 'tis true,
        But Snow White, living with the seven dwarfs,
        Is fairer than you.'

When she heard this, the queen flew into a rage and she set out for the dwarfs' house dressed as an old pedlar woman, with a basket of things for sale. When she arrived, she knocked on the door and sang out, 'Pretty things for sale. Pretty things for sale.'

Snow White opened the door and the wicked queen showed her a beautiful silk cord for lacing up her dress. Snow White loved it and the queen offered to help her tie it. But she pulled it so tight that the girl could hardly breathe and she fell down in a faint.

When the seven dwarfs came home, they were shocked to find Snow White lying still upon the floor. But when they saw her bodice tightly laced they quickly cut the cord, letting the girl breathe again.

Meanwhile, as soon as the queen reached her palace, she asked her mirror,
        'Mirror, mirror, on the wall,
        Who is the fairest one of all?'
And it answered as before,

'You, oh Queen, are fair, 'tis true,
But Snow White, living with the seven dwarfs,
Is fairer than you.'

The queen's blood ran cold and at once she prepared a poisoned comb. The next day she set out again, dressed as an old crone. Arriving at the little house, the queen knocked on the door, but Snow White called out, 'Go away, I won't let anyone in.'

'Just put your head out of the window and look at this lovely comb,' cried the queen.

Snow White leaned out of the window and in an instant, the wicked queen stuck the poisoned comb in her hair. Immediately the girl fell senseless to the floor.

As soon as the dwarfs came home, they realized that the wicked queen had called again. They found the poisoned comb and when they pulled it out, Snow White opened her eyes and told them what had happened.

When the wicked queen was back at her palace, she stood before her mirror and said with a smile,

'*Mirror, mirror, on the wall,*
Who is the fairest one of all?'

But the mirror answered as before,

'*You, oh Queen, are fair 'tis true,*
But Snow White, living with the seven dwarfs,
Is fairer than you.'

The queen shook with rage and vowed that she would make sure the girl was dead next time.

Early next morning, she set out, this time dressed as a village girl, carrying a basket of red apples. She knocked at the little door and called, 'Ripe apples. Big juicy apples.'

Snow White called from inside, 'Go away. I don't want any.'

'What's the matter?' laughed the woman. 'Are you frightened that I'm going to poison you? Look, I'll take a bite myself if you don't trust me.' With that, she took an apple from her basket, one half red, the other green. She bit into the green half before handing it to Snow White.

'Surely it must be safe,' thought the girl, and she took the apple. Little did she know that the wicked queen had poisoned the red half but not the green half. Hardly had she taken a bite, than she fell upon the floor as if she were dead.

With a laugh of triumph, the queen hurried back to her mirror and cried,

> *'Mirror, mirror, on the wall,*
> *Who is the fairest one of all?'*

The mirror replied,

> *'You, oh Queen, are the fairest in the land.'*

And the queen was content.

When the seven dwarfs found Snow White they could not rouse her. She remained quite lifeless. For three days and nights they wept over her, then laid her in a glass coffin so that everyone could see her.

One day, a prince came riding by. At once he fell in love with Snow White and begged the dwarfs to let him take her back to his palace. The dwarfs took pity on the prince and agreed to let him take her away.

The prince's servants went to take the coffin away. But, as they lifted it on to their shoulders, they knocked the poisoned piece of apple from Snow White's throat.

In a moment, Snow White opened her eyes, sat up and looked about her. 'Where am I?' she murmured.

'You are with me,' the prince cried with joy. 'I love you. Please come to my palace and be my wife.'

Snow White soon agreed, for she too had fallen in love. She bade farewell to the seven dwarfs, and rode off with the prince to his kingdom.

On the very day of the wedding the wicked queen spoke to her mirror:

> *'Mirror, mirror, on the wall,*
> *Who is the fairest one of all?'*

And she received an unexpected reply:

> *'You, oh Queen, are fair, 'tis true,*
> *But Snow White, the prince's bride*
> *Is fairer than you.'*

The queen was so angry that she dropped down dead in her rage. But Snow White and her prince lived happily ever after.

PUSS IN BOOTS

There was once a miller who had three sons. But one day he died and he left all he had to the three boys: his mill to the eldest, his donkey to the second son, and his cat to the youngest.

The youngest son felt quite sorry for himself. 'My brothers can make a living with what they've got, but what can I do with a cat?' he thought.

'Cheer up, Master,' said the cat. 'I can help you. Get me a sack and a pair of boots and you won't regret it.'

The young man was doubtful, but what was there to lose? So he made the cat a pair of smart boots, and fetched a sack.

When Puss had what he wanted, he went off with the sack over one shoulder to a rabbit field. Once there, he put green lettuce at the bottom of his sack, left it open before a rabbit hole and lay in wait. In no time at all a fat rabbit jumped into the sack and Puss carried him off to the king's palace.

Bowing low before the king, Puss said gravely, 'Your Majesty, I have brought you a gift from my noble lord the Duke of Carabas.'

The king was most grateful.

Next day, Puss in Boots took his sack to a cornfield and caught two partridges which he took to the king as before. So it continued each day until the king was sure that the Duke of Carabas must be a very wealthy man.

One day Puss heard that the king was to drive along the riverside with his lovely daughter.

'Master,' said Puss, 'do as I say and your fortune is made. Go bathing in the river and leave the rest to me.'

So the miller's son went off for a swim and, while he was bathing, Puss hid his clothes behind a bush. Soon the king and princess drove by in their coach.

'Help, help!' shouted Puss. 'The Duke of Carabas is drowning!'

As soon as he heard the shouts, the king looked from his carriage and recognized the cat who had brought him presents.

'Guards,' cried the king. 'Save the Duke of Carabas.'

While the guards pulled the surprised lad from the river, Puss told the king how thieves had stolen his master's clothes as he was bathing. He could not appear before the princess all wet and naked.

The king at once sent riders back to the palace to bring the richest suit from his own wardrobe. And when the young man had put on the royal clothes and brushed his hair, he looked for all the world like a handsome duke.

'What a fine young man,' thought the princess as she gazed out of the carriage. And to her father she said, 'Why don't we invite the duke to join us on our drive?'

Puss was pleased to see how well his plan was working and ran ahead to some peasants mowing a meadow. 'Hey you scoundrels,' he cried fiercely. 'I'll make mincemeat of you if you don't tell the king that this meadow belongs to the Duke of Carabas.'

So it was that, when the king drove by and asked whose meadow it was, the peasants all answered in chorus, 'It belongs to the Duke of Carabas!'

'You have a splendid field,' said the king to the miller's son.

In the meantime, Puss ran ahead until he came to a field where peasants were reaping wheat. 'Hey you villains,' he cried in his fiercest voice. 'If you don't tell the king this wheatfield belongs to the Duke of Carabas I'll grind your bones to dust.'

The peasants were so frightened by this threat that when the king drove by and wished to know who owned the wheatfield, they all called out in chorus, 'It belongs to the Duke of Carabas!'

The king was even more impressed. 'You have an excellent field of wheat,' he said to the miller's son, who kept silent as before.

Puss, meanwhile, had run on to tell everyone he met what they should say: this field and that belonged to the Duke of Carabas. And the king was quite astonished at the duke's fine estate.

In truth, the lands belonged to a terrible giant who lived in a castle along the way. The cruel tyrant kept all his servants in fear and trembling, for he had a magic power: he could turn himself into whatever shape he liked. No one was safe from him.

PUSS IN BOOTS

It was to the giant's castle that Puss in Boots was now leading the king's coach, though he took good care to reach it first, some way before the coach.

Putting on his boldest face, Puss marched up to the castle and announced to the guards that he had come to pay his respects to the noble lord.

The giant received him as politely as a giant can, and asked him his business.

'I am here, dear sir,' Puss replied, 'because I hear you can change yourself into anything you like: a lion, a tiger or even an elephant.'

'True,' the giant said.

Puss looked doubtful.

'Don't you believe me?' the giant roared. 'Then watch this,' and he became a lion there and then.

Face to face with a lion, even Puss was scared. He quickly scrambled up into the rafters, out of reach of the lion's claws.

Only when the giant had turned back into his usual self did Puss come down, confessing how frightened he had been. 'But my dear sir,' he said, 'it may be easy to turn into a big beast like a lion, but can you change into something as small as a mouse? I think that's impossible.'

The giant scowled. 'Impossible?' he roared. 'Just watch this,' and at once he was a mouse scampering along the floor.

That was just what Puss wanted. He did what any cat would do. He pounced on the mouse and killed it on the spot, putting an end to the cruel giant.

By this time, the king and princess, and Puss's master had arrived at the castle. The moment the cat heard the carriage wheels trundling over the drawbridge he ran outside and announced in a loud voice, 'Welcome, Your Majesty, to the castle of my lord, the Duke of Carabas.'

The king's mouth dropped open in surprise. 'What?' he said, turning to the miller's son. 'Does this fine castle belong to you? I've never seen anything so splendid in my life. Such a moat, such a drawbridge, such battlements.'

69

Bowing modestly, the young man followed closely behind Puss in Boots, and led his royal guests into the castle. They entered a grand hall where a fine banquet was being laid out on Puss's orders. The oaken tables were groaning under the wonderful food and wine.

As the meal progressed, it did not take the miller's son long to pick up royal airs and graces. The king and princess were so charmed by his good manners and, of course, his wealth, that after his sixth or seventh glass of wine, the king proposed a toast. 'To the Duke of Carabas to whom I offer my daughter in marriage.'

Of course, the young man agreed immediately to the proposal, and the happy pair were married that very day.

As for Puss in Boots, he became a noble lord and lived a life of ease, hunting mice only when the fancy took him.

BEAUTY AND THE BEAST

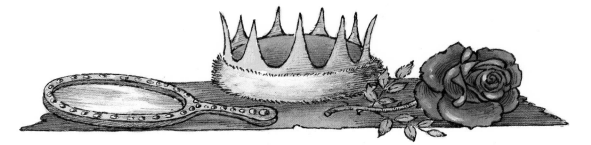

Once upon a time there was a rich merchant who had three daughters. One day, as he was leaving to trade his wares across the seas, he asked his daughters what gifts they would like him to bring back. One said she would like a crystal mirror, the second asked for a golden crown, but the youngest, Beauty, asked only for a dark red rose.

The merchant sailed to foreign lands. He sold his wares and bought the mirror and the crown. But nowhere could he find a dark red rose, and he had to return home without one.

When the merchant was nearly home, his ship was wrecked on a strange land. It was covered by a dense, dark forest and the merchant had to push his way through the trees. After walking all day long, he came at last to a splendid palace, and in the gardens, growing upon a grassy mound, he saw a beautiful dark red rose. Its fragrance filled the air with sweet perfume.

Thinking of Beauty, the merchant ran at once and picked the rose. At that moment, there appeared before him an ugly creature. It roared in a savage voice, 'How dare you pick my rose? I will kill you this instant.'

The poor merchant fell to his knees, crying that the rose was for his youngest, fairest daughter, not for himself.

'I will spare you,' said the Beast, 'if within three days your daughter comes here in your stead. But she must come of her own free will.' With that, he gave the merchant a gold ring and the unlucky man found himself transported home, still holding the beautiful rose. There, amidst his family, he related his adventure.

Without a second thought, Beauty agreed to save her father and go to the Beast's far-off palace. As her father bowed his head in grief, she put on the ring and vanished with her rose.

In no time at all she was within the palace gardens, standing before the grassy mound. The rose flew from her hands and settled in its former bed, blooming more richly than before.

As she entered the palace, sweet music played on invisible strings and food was served by unseen hands. Words of fire appeared upon the marble wall:

Welcome, Beauty, have no fear,
You are queen and mistress here.

Beauty ate the food but found no one to thank. She made her way to a fine chamber and slept soundly on a swansdown bed.

Thus it was that Beauty came to live in the enchanted palace. Each day silk robes were laid out for her. Each day she rode through the forest in a golden carriage. She read and played music and embroidered as the fancy took her.

Time passed, and as she became used to her new life Beauty slowly lost her fear. Daily she grew fonder of the Beast although she never met him. He made her life as happy as he could, and soon she longed to hear his voice and talk with him.

So, one evening, she spoke aloud and begged the Beast to talk to her. But he would not answer, afraid that his savage voice would frighten her. Finally, unable to resist her pleas any longer, he made a message appear on the marble wall:

In the gardens at midday,

Beauty, you must say,

Talk to me, my humble slave.

Beauty could not conceal her joy. Long before midday she was seated in the gardens, repeating the words she had read.

As the sun rose overhead, there came at last a piteous sigh from behind a nearby bush. Then a snarling voice made her shake from head to toe. But she mastered her fear and, as she listened to the Beast's words, so wise and kind, her heart grew lighter.

From then on, they talked throughout the day and Beauty soon had no fear of the Beast's savage voice. She then longed to see him and begged him not to hide from her any more. For a long time, the Beast refused, afraid that his terrible form would scare her and make her hate him. One day, however, he gave in. 'I will grant your wish,' he said, 'though I know it will destroy us both. Come to the gardens at dusk and say: "Show yourself to me, dear friend."'

Unafraid, Beauty went to the gardens at dusk and, as the sun was sinking low, she called softly, 'Show yourself to me, dear friend.'

The Beast appeared, quickly crossing the path at the end of the gardens. When Beauty saw him she let out a cry of horror and fainted upon the spot. When she awoke, she heard the Beast sobbing as if his heart would break. She felt ashamed and spoke up strongly, trying to conceal her fear. 'Do not cry, dear friend. True beauty lies within, not in one's looks.'

After that, they walked and talked together. They wandered through the gardens and drove in the dark forest in a horseless carriage. Once, the Beast asked Beauty to marry him but she was not brave enough to do that.

One night, Beauty dreamed that her father was lying ill. When she told the Beast the next morning, he said at once, 'Go home, my dear. But please heed my words. If you do not return within a week I shall die of a broken heart.' With that he put the gold ring upon her finger.

Immediately Beauty found herself at home. Her father was indeed ill, but he was happy to see her and soon regained his health.

Beauty's two sisters grew jealous of her happiness as they both lived in boredom with their husbands. So when the hour drew near for her return, they begged her not to go, distracting her with games and happy talk. Poor Beauty could not tear herself away and a whole week passed.

Then, one night, Beauty dreamed that the Beast lay dying. When she awoke, she quickly put the gold ring on her finger and found herself at once in the palace gardens. All was still. No one answered when she called. In fear, she searched the palace and the gardens for the Beast and found him at last, lying on the ground near the grassy mound, the dark red rose in his paw.

Gently, Beauty tried to wake him, but he was too weak to even open his eyes. She cried with shame and pity and put her arms around his neck. She kissed him tenderly and a single tear fell on his head. 'Please don't die, Beast,' she wept. 'Live and be my husband.'

In an instant, light glowed all around and music played. The Beast awoke and Beauty saw that he was no longer ugly, but was a young and handsome prince.

The prince told Beauty his story.

'When I was young, an evil demon turned me into a beast as revenge upon my father, the king. For twenty years I have suffered. Only when a girl loved me in spite of my ugliness, would the spell be broken. You have broken the spell, Beauty, because you grew to love me truly.'

The very next day, Beauty and the prince were married. A grand wedding was held amid great rejoicing. And their happiness, built upon the goodness of their hearts, was complete.

THE THREE
LITTLE PIGS

Once upon a time there was an old mother pig and her three children. Times were hard and since she did not have enough to feed the little pigs she had to send them into the world to seek their fortune.

The first little pig went down the road and after a time met a man with a bundle of straw.

'Good-day, man,' said the little pig. 'Will you give me some straw to build a house?'

'Yes, of course, little pig,' the man replied, and he gave the pig an armful of straw.

The pig went off with his bundle, chose a spot for his house and built himself a house of straw. He lived inside, snug and warm.

Not long after, a wolf came along. He knocked at the door and called out, 'Little pig, little pig, let me come in.'

'No, no,' said the pig. 'Not by the hair on my chinny chin chin, I won't let you in.'

To which the wolf replied, 'Then I'll huff and I'll puff and I'll blow your house in.'

And he did. He huffed and he puffed and he blew the house in. Then he ate up the first little pig.

Meanwhile, the second little pig set off to seek his fortune. He had not gone far before he met a man with a bundle of sticks.

'Good-day, man,' he said. 'Will you give me some sticks to build a house?'

'Yes, of course, little pig,' the man replied, and he gave the pig an armful of sticks.

Off went the little pig with his bundle and he built a house of sticks. He lived inside, snug and warm.

Not long after the wolf came along. He knocked at the door and called out, 'Little pig, little pig, let me come in.'

'No, no,' said the pig. 'Not by the hair on my chinny chin chin, I won't let you in.'

To which the wolf replied, 'Then I'll huff and I'll puff and I'll blow your house in.'

And he did. He huffed and he puffed, and he puffed and he huffed, and he blew the house in. Then he immediately ate up the second little pig.

Some time later the third little pig was walking down the road on his way to the local market when he met a man with a load of bricks.

'Good-day, man,' he said. 'Will you give me some bricks to build a house?'

'Yes, of course, little pig,' the man replied, and he gave the pig a pile of bricks.

Off went the pig and he built a house of bricks. He lived inside, snug and warm.

Later that day the wolf came along, knocked at the door and called out, 'Little pig, little pig, let me come in.'

'No, no,' said the pig. 'Not by the hair on my chinny chin chin, I won't let you in.'

To which the wolf replied, 'Then I'll huff and I'll puff and I'll blow your house in.'

So he huffed and he puffed, and he huffed and he puffed, and he huffed and he puffed, but he could not blow the house in. Finally, the wolf grew tired and called out, 'Little pig, little pig, I know where there's a field of turnips.'

The little pig was curious. 'Where is it?' he asked.

'Down by Farmer Smith's meadow,' said the wolf. 'If you'll be ready tomorrow morning I'll take you there.'

'What time will you come?' asked the little pig.

'At eight o'clock.'

'Very well, I'll be ready.'

Now that little pig was very clever. He got up at seven and was out and back with the turnips before the wolf arrived at his door. So when the wolf knocked and asked if he was ready, the little pig answered, 'I went out to Farmer Smith's meadow before breakfast, thank you, and I have a whole potful of turnips for my dinner.'

That made the wolf very angry. But he was even more determined to catch the little pig and he called out, 'Little pig, little pig, I know where there's a tree with juicy red apples.'

'Where is it?' asked the little pig.

'Down in Farmer Brown's back garden. I'll call for you tomorrow and we can go there together, if you like.'

'What time will you come?' asked the pig.

'At seven o'clock.'

'Very well, I'll be ready.'

Next morning the little pig was up at six and off to Farmer Brown's garden. But this time he had to climb the apple tree and pick the apples. Just as he was about to climb down again he saw the wolf approaching. What was he to do?

The wolf came up and stood beneath the tree. 'Well, well, little pig, fancy you getting here so early. Are the apples tasty?' he asked.

'Oh yes,' said the pig. 'They are delicious. I'll throw one down for you to try.' He threw the apple as far as he could, right to the bottom of the garden, and while the wolf was fetching it he scrambled down from the tree and ran home as fast as his legs would carry him.

How cross the wolf was at being tricked again, and now he was even more determined to catch the little pig. So, next day, he came again to the house of bricks, knocked at the door, and called out, 'Little pig, little pig, there's a fair on the common today. Would you like to go this afternoon?'

'Yes, I would,' said the pig. 'What time will you come for me?'

'At three o'clock.'

'Very well, I'll be ready.'

As usual the little pig set off early. He went to the fair, had a good time and bought a barrel to keep his apples in. He was on his way home, when who should he see at the bottom of the hill but the wolf! Not knowing what to do, he hid inside his barrel. As he climbed inside he set the barrel rolling down the hill, faster and faster, heading straight for the wolf.

It scared the wolf out of his skin. Thinking a monster was after him, he took to his heels and ran right back home again, shivering with fright.

Later that day, when he had recovered, he paid another visit to the little pig's house, knocked on the door and called out, 'Do you know, pig, I was going to the fair when a terrible monster rushed down the hill straight at me. I barely escaped with my life.'

How the little pig laughed. 'That was me,' he said, and he explained what had happened.

The wolf hopped up and down with rage, shaking his fist at the locked door. 'I shall catch you and eat you up if it's the last thing I do,' he roared. 'I'm going to climb down the chimney.'

On hearing that, the little pig quickly put a potful of water on the fire and stoked up the flames, so that by the time the wolf had climbed up on to the roof, the water was bubbling and boiling.

When he slid down the chimney, the wolf fell straight into the piping hot water. At once, the clever little pig brought the lid of the pot down hard and from that moment on, he lived in peace and comfort for the rest of his days.

CINDERELLA

Once upon a time there was a rich man who lived happily with his wife and daughter. But the good wife died and the man married a widow who had two daughters just like herself: vain and ugly.

No sooner was the wedding over than the stepmother began to illtreat her husband's daughter. The poor girl had to scrub the floors, wash the dishes, dust the stairs, make the beds and rake out the fire.

In the evening, when her work was done, the girl would sit in the chimney corner of the kitchen, close to the warm cinders of the fire. Because of this the two sisters called her Cinders or Cinderella. Yet even in her rags she was a hundred times prettier than them.

One day the king's son announced he was going to have a ball, and he invited all the high society of the town. Of course, the two ugly sisters were to go, and for weeks they talked of nothing else.

Poor Cinderella was kept busy washing, ironing, and starching their clothes. Then on the day of the ball she had to curl their hair and dab rouge and powder on their cheeks. Do you think they were grateful? Not a bit. As she did their hair, they poked fun at her: 'I bet you wish you were going to the ball, Cinderella. Can you imagine? Cinders at a ball! What would the prince say?' How they laughed at her.

At last it was time to leave for the ball. Off the two sisters went in their carriage, while Cinderella sadly watched them out of sight. Then she cleaned up the house and went to sit on her little chimney stool by the fire where she began to cry.

Suddenly, a beautiful lady appeared. It was Cinderella's fairy godmother.

'Why are you crying?' the fairy asked kindly.

'I would like so much to go to the ball,' Cinderella answered.

'Well now,' said the fairy, 'run into the garden and fetch the largest pumpkin you can find.'

Cinderella brought the finest, ripest, roundest, orange pumpkin. Scooping out the inside, the fairy then tapped the shell with her magic wand. Instantly, the pumpkin became a golden coach.

'Now fetch the mousetrap from the pantry,' said the fairy.

Cinderella found six mice scrambling about inside the cage. She opened the mouse-trap door and her fairy godmother tapped each mouse gently on the head as it ran out. In an instant each one became a splendid horse. So the coach had a team of six mouse-coloured horses. All they needed now was a driver.

'Shall we see if the rat-trap has a rat?' Cinderella asked. 'We could make a coachman out of him,' and she ran to fetch the trap.

Of the three fat rats within the trap, the fairy chose the longest-whiskered one. With a tap of the magic wand she made him into a fat jolly coachman, clothed in velvet with long whiskers.

'Now you shall go to the ball,' said the fairy. 'You have a
coach, six horses and a driver to take you there.'

'Oh, thank you,' said Cinderella. 'But I can't go to the ball in
this shabby dress.'

The fairy smiled. Touching Cinderella with her magic wand,
she turned rags to riches in an instant. The sooty, ragged dress
became a gown of silk and lace, sparkling with precious jewels.
Cinderella's long hair shone like sunshine and on her dainty feet
were the prettiest glass slippers ever seen.

Cinderella went off joyfully to the ball. But as she was leaving,
her fairy godmother said, 'Remember one thing well: be home
before the clock strikes twelve, not a minute later. The magic only
lasts till then.'

When Cinderella arrived at the palace, the prince was informed
that an unknown princess had arrived. He came out himself to greet

her and led her on his arm into the ballroom past the assembled guests. The dancing stopped and the music ceased, while everyone stood and stared at the beautiful princess. The prince led Cinderella to the place of honour and sat her down. Then he asked her to dance.

She danced. Oh how she danced. She was so graceful that she was even more admired. She and the prince whirled about the ballroom to gasps of wonder from the crowd. The prince would not leave her side. He danced with no one else and confessed how much he loved her. Cinderella was so happy that time slipped by unnoticed and she forgot all about her godmother's words. It was only when she heard the palace clock striking that she remembered.

One, two, three . . .

'It must surely be eleven,' she thought.

But no, the clock struck twelve times. Midnight!

Cinderella jumped up and fled as swiftly as a deer. Although the prince sprang up in pursuit he could not catch her. All he found was one glass slipper upon the palace steps. The guards were questioned. Had they seen a lady pass? No, no one had seen a beautiful princess, only a shabby girl in a ragged dress.

Cinderella arrived home quite out of breath, having run all the way. Nothing remained of her coach and horses, her jolly driver or all her finery. They had all vanished in a puff of smoke. All that was left were the two glass slippers: one on her foot and one with the prince.

A few days later a proclamation was heard:

'Hear Ye! Hear Ye! Hear Ye! His Royal Highness will wed the maid whose foot fits the slipper.' And the little glass slipper was paraded through the town on a velvet cushion.

First, all the princesses from miles around tried it on, then duchesses and ladies of the court. All in vain. Finally, it was brought to each house in the land and at last it came to Cinderella's home.

The stepsisters tried it on and Cinderella watched as they squeezed and pushed. But their feet were much too big.

'May I try it on?' she asked politely.

Cinderella's sisters burst out laughing. But the footman said, 'My orders are to ask every girl to try on the slipper,' he said. 'Sit down, young miss, and hold out your foot.'

The little slipper slid on easily, as if it was made for her alone.
Then Cinderella pulled the matching slipper from her apron. Just at
that moment her Fairy Godmother appeared and, with a touch of her
magic wand, changed Cinderella's rags to riches as before.
Thereupon even the ugly sisters recognized the fair princess of the
palace ball.

Without more ado, Cinderella was taken to the prince and they
were married that very day. And, since she was as good as she was
beautiful, she brought her sisters to live with her at the palace.
Within a time they learned to be more loving, and both found good
husbands in their turn.

TOM THUMB

There was once a poor peasant and his wife. As they were sitting one evening by the fire, the peasant muttered sadly to his wife, 'What a shame we have no children of our own. Our home is quiet and empty, while others are so full of fun.'

'Yes,' sighed his wife. 'I wish we had a little boy even if he was no bigger than my thumb. We would still love him with all our hearts.'

A wizard or a fairy must have heard her wish, for some time later she did have a child. It was a little boy who was perfect in every way, yet no bigger than a thumb. His parents were content. 'Well, our wish is granted,' they said, 'and, small as he is, we shall love him with all our hearts.'

Because he was so small they called him little Tom Thumb, and no matter how much they gave him to eat, he grew no taller than the day he was born. All the same, he was a clever lad, and never idle.

One day, the peasant was making ready to go into the forest to cut some wood. 'If only I had someone to bring my cart to collect the wood,' he thought to himself. 'It would save me a lot of time.'

'I'll do it, Father,' piped up little Tom Thumb. 'Just tell Mother to sit me in the horse's ear and I'll tell it where to go. Leave it to me.'

His father was doubtful, but when the peasant's wife harnessed the horse she sat Tom in the horse's ear. Then, off went the horse and cart to shrill cries of, 'Giddy up. Whoah. Gee up.'

All went well until they turned the corner of the track, passing two travellers.

'Well I'll be darned,' said one. 'Did you see what I saw? A horse with no driver.'

'That's queer,' said the other. 'Let's follow it.'

The cart trundled on into the forest and arrived at last to where Tom's father was cutting wood.

'Here I am, Father,' called Tom. 'Help me down.'

So the peasant lifted the tiny boy out of the horse's ear and set him down on a log. When the two men saw the boy they were astonished. 'Listen,' whispered one. 'That tiny fellow could make us a fortune if we put him in a circus.'

Going to the peasant, the men said, 'Sell us your boy. We'll treat him well and make him famous.'

Of course, the peasant had no wish to part with Tom Thumb, not for all the gold in the world. But the boy climbed up to his father's shoulder and whispered in his ear, 'Do as they say, Father. I'll run away from them and be back in no time.'

So the poor peasant sold the boy for a hundred gold coins, and off the two men went with Tom Thumb sitting on the brim of one man's hat.

On and on they walked until it grew dark. Then the man took off his hat and set Tom upon the ground. While the men sat at the edge of a field, eating their supper, Tom crept off unnoticed across the field. Soon he found a little mouse hole and crawled into it, calling out, 'Goodbye, gentlemen. You'll have to go to the circus without me.'

Although they poked sticks into the hole, the men could not reach Tom, who crawled farther down his underground tunnel. In the end they had to give up and went off very cross.

Soon after, Tom heard two more men approaching, talking of robbing a rich squire.

'How are we to get our hands on his gold?' said one.

'I can tell you,' came a tiny voice, which was Tom's.

'Who spoke there?' cried a robber, getting quite a fright.

The two men began to search about for the voice and finally found Tom beside the mouse hole.

'Now how can you help us?' asked the robbers.

'Take me along with you to the manor house,' said Tom, 'and when we get there I'll squeeze through the bars of the Squire's window and pass out the gold to you.'

The men could scarcely believe their luck, and one of them picked Tom up and put him into his pocket. When they reached the manor, Tom squeezed into the house and began to shout with all his might, 'Thieves! Thieves!' He made such a racket that he woke up the servants who caught the robbers and took them off to prison.

Tom made his way into the barn and lay down in some warm hay, intending to return home in the morning, but it was not to be.

Early next day, when the milkmaid came to feed the cows, she picked up Tom's bundle of hay and before he knew it he was inside a cow's mouth being eaten for breakfast.

Dodging in and out of the munching teeth, he tried hard to scramble out of the cow's mouth, but mouthfuls of hay kept pushing him back again. Finally, he slipped down the cow's throat, all the way to its stomach.

'Help, help,' he shouted.

His cries so alarmed the milkmaid that she ran, screaming, to the squire. 'The cow is talking! The cow is talking!' she cried.

That brought the squire running to the cowshed, just in time to hear Tom shout, 'The hay is crushing me. Stop it! Help!'

So scared was the squire that he thought the cow must be bewitched. 'The cow is talking! The cow is talking!' he cried. He called the farmlands and he had it killed forthwith.

Snorting and sneezing, and not smelling very sweetly, Tom climbed his way out into the fresh air. But just then, a hungry fox ran by and swallowed him whole.

Again Tom ended up in an animal's belly. But the cheerful little lad did not lose heart. 'Hey, Foxie,' he cried. 'I know where there's plenty of food to be had.'

Frightened at first by the voice from its belly, the fox soon got over the shock and asked where it could find the food. Clever Tom directed the fox straight to his father's house, through the pantry window and in amongst the bacon, sausages, cakes and cream. The greedy fox quickly gulped down all the food in the pantry. It grew so fat that it could not squeeze out through the pantry window.

That was what Tom was counting on. He began to yell and bawl as hard as he could.

'Not so loud,' said the Fox, 'or you'll wake the household.'

But Tom shouted even louder from inside the Fox.

The noise finally woke up his father and mother who came running downstairs to see what all the row was about. Imagine their surprise when they found the talking fox.

As soon as he heard his father's voice, Tom Thumb shouted out, 'Father, it's me, little Tom Thumb. I'm inside the fox.'

Without more ado, his father killed the fox and rescued the little boy.

'Where have you been?' he asked. 'We've been so worried about you.'

'Oh Father, I've been down a mouse hole, inside a cow's stomach and into a fox's belly. I've had enough of travelling. I'll never leave you again.'

Nor did he. His parents washed him clean, made him a brand new suit and never let him out of their sight again.

THE PIED PIPER

A long time ago, in the town of Hamelin, there once was a plague of rats. The rats were all colours and sizes and they ran boldly, in broad daylight, through the streets and all over the houses. People could not put a foot down anywhere without treading on a rat. And, when they got dressed in the mornings, they found rats in their petticoats and trousers, in their pockets and their boots. They had tried cats, dogs, poison and traps to get rid of the rats but nothing seemed to work.

One day, there arrived in Hamelin a long, thin man. He was dressed in a scarlet and yellow cloak and a pointed hat and he was playing a pipe. He sent word to the Town Council that, if they made it worth his while, he would rid them of all their rats by nightfall.

The Council was willing to try anything and so a price was agreed upon — one penny a head. The stranger then went to the market-place. He stood in the square, put his pipe to his lips and started to play a tune. It was a slow, caressing sound that gradually picked up pace until its lively notes drifted to the farthest alleys of the town.

Soon the rats came out. They came from the bottom of the cellars, the tops of the attics and from all the nooks and crannies of the houses. They scurried into the streets and ran towards the market-place.

When the square was full of rats, the Pied Piper began to walk out of the town towards the river, still playing his pipe. The rats followed him and still more filled the square and hurried after him. When he reached the riverside, the Piper halted. But all the rats ran on past him, plunged head first into the river and disappeared.

The Piper, having thus finished his business, went to bed in an inn. And for the first time in three months, the people of Hamelin slept soundly all through the night.

Next morning, at nine o'clock, the Piper went to the town hall and demanded his due — a penny a head.

'But where are the heads?' asked the Lord Mayor with a smirk. 'No heads, no reward.'

The Piper was not expecting such trickery. He paled with anger and his eyes flashed fire. 'If you want the heads,' he said, 'go and fish them out of the river.' With that, he turned on his heel and left the town hall without another word.

When the townspeople heard of the trick, they rubbed their hands and laughed at the Piper. Now they would not have to pay extra taxes to pay him for his work.

The next day was a Sunday and in the morning all the people of Hamelin went to church, leaving their children at home. They never suspected the terrible shock that awaited them on their return. Their children had disappeared.

The parents searched everywhere but could not find a single child. Finally they saw a sad lame boy limping through the east gate of the town.

This is the tale he told.

While the parents were at church, a wonderful music had rung out through the town and all the girls and boys had rushed out of doors.

They had run to the market-place where they had found the Pied
Piper playing his pipe. When all the children had gathered, the
Piper had turned and walked out through the east gate towards the
hill outside the town. All the children had followed, running,
singing, and dancing to the sound of the music.

As they had approached the hill, a door in the hillside had
opened and all the children had passed through behind the Piper.
Then the door had closed again. Only the lame boy had remained
outside; he had not been able to keep up with the others and had
cried when he saw the door close before he could reach it.

When they heard the boy's story, the people rushed with stakes
and sticks to the hillside where they poked and prised till late
evening, trying to find the door through which their children had
disappeared. But it was in vain, and at last, when it was pitch black,
they returned empty-handed to Hamelin. Too late, they regretted
that the Lord Mayor had tricked the Pied Piper out of his payment.
They never saw their children again.

THE PRINCESS AND THE PEA

Once upon a time there was a prince who wished to marry a real princess. He travelled all around the world to find one, and during his journey, he found many. But there was always something wrong. He could not put his finger on it, but first one thing, then another seemed not quite right. In the end, tired and disappointed, he returned to his palace, unhappy that he had not found a real princess to be his wife.

One evening, shortly after his return, a raging storm arose, making the windows of the palace rattle and the chimneys howl. The rain poured down, thunder boomed and lightning flashed.

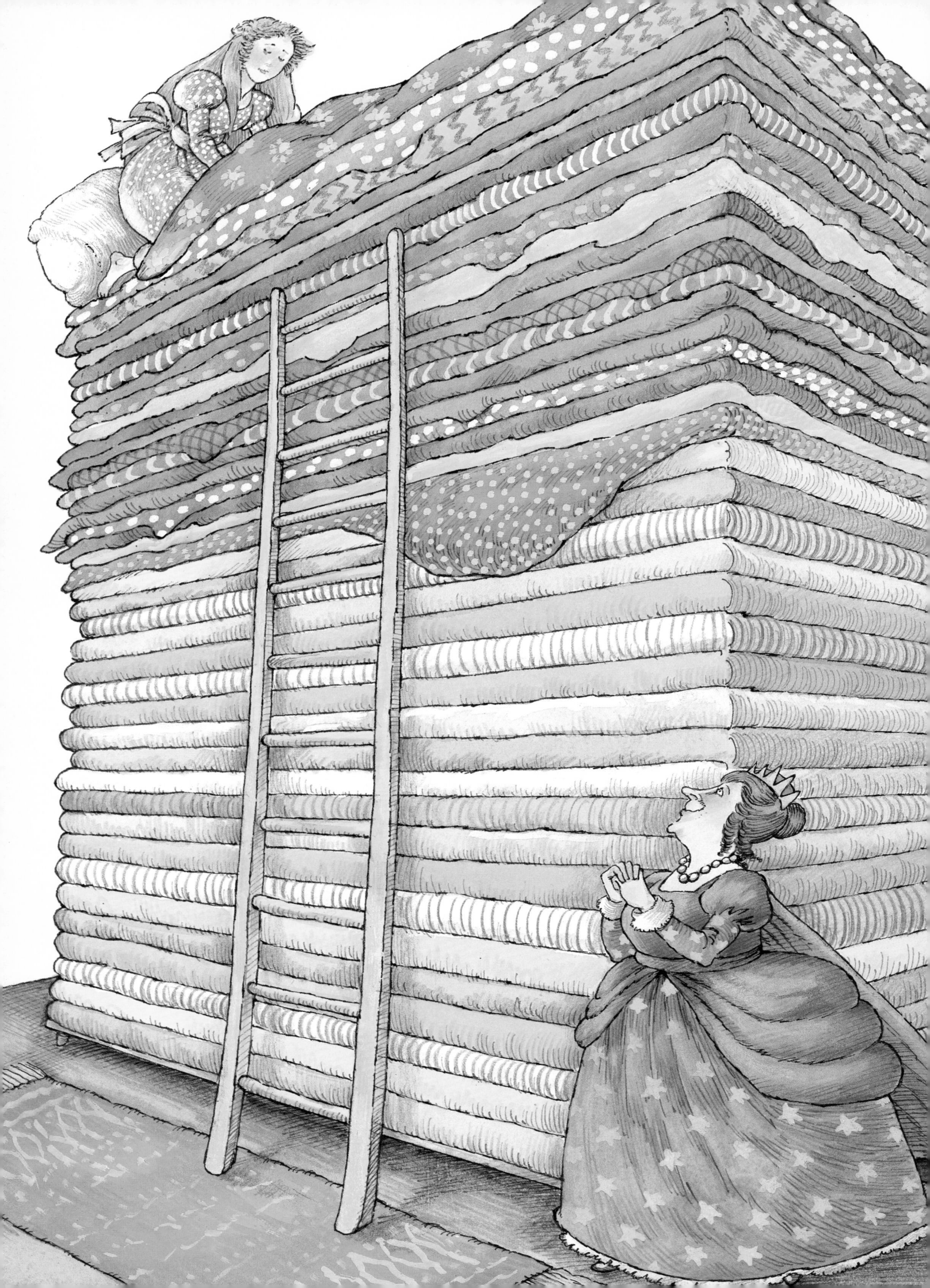

All at once, there was a loud knocking on the door, and the old king, the prince's father, went to open it. Who should be standing there but a fair princess, or so she claimed. But the wind and rain had turned her into a sorry sight. Her hair hung limp and wet, drops of water dripped from her nose, and her once-fine clothes clung like rags to her body. But she said she was a real princess.

'We'll soon see about that!' muttered the old queen to herself. She went quietly to the spare bedroom, took all the bedclothes off the bed, and put a little pea upon the bedstead. Then she laid twenty mattresses one upon the other above the little pea, and put twenty eiderdowns upon the mattresses. This was the bed the princess was to sleep in.

Next morning, when the fair princess came down to breakfast, the king, queen and prince looked at her closely, for the queen had told the others what she had done.

'Excuse me my dear,' said the old queen. 'How did you spend the night? I trust you slept well.'

The princess looked at her with tired eyes and said with a sigh, 'Forgive me for saying, but I had an awful night. I scarcely slept a wink the whole night through. Goodness knows what was in my bed, but it felt so hard and lumpy underneath me. I'm black and blue all over.'

Three broad smiles spread around the breakfast table. It was plain that the lady was a real princess. For she had felt the little pea through twenty mattresses and twenty eiderdowns. No one but a true princess could have such tender feelings.

The prince was delighted. Quite sure that he had found a real princess at last, he soon made her his wife. As for the little pea, it was placed on a marble stand and displayed in the Royal Museum. It can be seen there to this day if, that is, it has not been lost.

THE ELVES AND THE SHOEMAKER

Once upon a time there lived a kind old shoemaker and his wife. They were very poor, and one day all they had left to eat in their pantry was a single loaf of bread. When that was gone they would surely starve to death, for it was months since the shoemaker had sold a pair of shoes.

The good man had only enough leather left for one pair of shoes, though he had no customers to buy them. All the same, he cut out the leather for shoes before going to bed that night and placed it on his work-bench, ready to sew and stitch next morning. Then he and his wife had a slice of bread and cup of water, said their prayers and went upstairs to bed.

In the morning, the shoemaker came downstairs, but just as he was about to sit down to work he noticed a pair of shoes neatly stitched and sewn from the leather patterns he had left last night. He stared at the work-bench in disbelief. 'Look at this, wife,' he shouted. 'Someone's playing tricks on me, though I cannot think who.'

He inspected the shoes from every side: right and left, uppers and soles. No, there was not a stitch or nail out of place, not a scrap of difference between left and right. Both shoes were as well made as he had ever seen.

That clearly was his lucky day, for later a customer came in, tried on the shoes and found they fitted perfectly. It seemed as if they had been made to order. So delighted was the customer that he willingly paid a handsome sum for the splendid shoes.

With the money the shoes had earned, the shoemaker was able to buy enough food for his wife and himself for several days. He also bought some leather to make two more pairs of shoes.

By the time he returned with the new leather, it was already getting late. He only had time to cut out the shapes for the shoes, then he left them on his bench, ready to make up next morning.

He and his wife had three slices of bread and dripping washed down with ale before saying their prayers and going to bed. After a sound night's sleep, the shoemaker came downstairs, early, to make a start on the shoes. But there was no need. To his astonishment, two pairs of shoes lay ready and waiting on his bench, just as neatly stitched and sewn as before.

'Wife,' he called, 'come quickly. Someone's done it again, though, bless me, I don't know who.'

They both stared in amazement. But there were the shoes and two customers were already knocking on the door. Again the shoes fitted perfectly, as if they had been ordered specially. And the two customers paid a large sum in gratitude.

Now the shoemaker had enough money to buy a week's supply of food, and leather for four pairs of shoes. He cut out the leather before going to bed that night and placed it on his work-bench. Then he and his wife had four slices of bread and dripping washed down with ale before saying their prayers and going up the stairs to bed.

Next morning, he found the shoes all done: four pairs neatly stitched, hammered and sewn. Customers were queueing at the door, as news of the shoemaker's craft was spreading through the town.

And so it went on. Each day he would buy more leather, shape and cut it overnight, say his prayers and go to bed. In the morning, no matter how many pairs he had cut out the night before, there they were, all in a row, stitched and sewn, and perfectly finished.

Since no one owned up to the work, the shoemaker and his wife became more and more puzzled. One evening, just before Christmas, they were sitting before the fire, when the shoemaker said to his wife, 'Shall we stay up tonight and keep watch? It's time we found out who is helping us.'

His wife agreed, lit a candle and, together, they hid behind a curtain in the corner of the room. They peered through a crack and waited to see what would happen.

For a while nothing was heard. Time passed and both were growing drowsy. But, on the stroke of midnight, there was a rattling and a rustling in the chimney and down came two funny little elves dressed in rags. They landed on the hearth with a bump, but bounced up at once like rubber balls.

They skipped over to the shoemaker's bench and set to work: stitching, sewing, hammering. They worked so swiftly and skilfully that the shoemaker was astonished, and they did not stop working till all the shoes were finished. Then, putting the pairs of shoes neatly in a row, they climbed down from the bench and scrambled back up the chimney.

'Well I never,' said the shoemaker's wife as soon as the elves had gone. 'Those two little fellows have made us rich, yet their own clothes are all in rags. In the depths of winter too. I think we should do something for them to show our gratitude.'

'Indeed, indeed,' her husband agreed.

'I'll tell you what,' she went on. 'I'll make them each a little vest and shirt. I'll make two smart waistcoats, two jackets and two pairs of trousers. Then I'll knit a little pair of socks for each of them. In the meantime, you can set to work and make them two tiny pairs of shoes.'

The two of them got down to work at once.

The sewing, knitting, stitching and hammering took quite some time, for they wanted the clothes and shoes to be just right. At last, on Christmas Eve, each single item was complete.

The shoemaker and his wife laid out their presents for the little elves all together on the work-bench where they normally left the cut-out shapes. In expectation, they then hid themselves, as before, behind a curtain in a corner of the room.

'I wonder what they'll say?' said the shoemaker.

'I hope the clothes will fit them all right,' replied his wife anxiously.

Again they had to wait till midnight before there came a rattling and a rustling in the chimney, and down slid the elves, landing on the hearth with a bump. They were just as ragged, yet as lively as before, and they bounced up at once. This time, however, when they looked on the work-bench, they could hardly believe their eyes. There was no cut-out leather for them to make shoes out of. There were only two little outfits of clothes laid out neatly on the bench.

Of course, it did not take them long to realize who they were for. There were two little vests and shirts, two smart waistcoats and little jackets, two pairs of trousers, two pairs of knitted socks and two pairs of tiny shoes. It was all for them!

Throwing off their rags, they quickly put on the new clothes, giggling and singing all the while:

> 'Now we're elves so fine to see,
> No longer will we cobblers be.'

Over and over again, they sang the song. Then they opened the door, danced out into the street and away in a shaft of moonbeams.

After that night they never called again, but it did not matter. The shoemaker's shoes were so popular that people came from far and near to buy them. And from that time forth, he and his wife lived in peace and comfort for the rest of their days.

THE FROG PRINCE

Long ago, when wishes came true and elves played merry pranks, there lived a king with three beautiful daughters. The youngest princess was the fairest of them all: brighter than the summer sun, paler than the moon. On summer days she would go into the shady forest and sit beside a cool pond, dreaming dreams or playing with her golden ball.

One day, as she was playing with the ball beside the pond, she dropped it and it rolled into the water. Being gold, it sank right to the bottom.

Since the pond was too deep for her to see the bottom, the princess knew her ball was lost forever and she began to cry, so hard you would think her heart would break.

All of a sudden, in the midst of all her tears, she heard a voice coming from the very depths of the pond.

'What's the matter, dear princess? Your tears would melt a heart of stone.'

When the princess stared into the water, she was startled to see a slimy frog pop his green head out of the pond. It was evidently this frog who had spoken.

'Oh, it's only you,' she cried. 'If you must know, I'm crying because I've lost my ball in the pond.'

'Never mind,' the frog said kindly. 'I can fetch it for you. But what will you give me in return?'

'Oh, I'd give anything to have my ball back,' she said. 'You can have any of my robes or pearls or even my golden crown.'

'I have no need of your robes or pearls or golden crown,' said he. 'But if you will promise to love me, let me sit at your side, eat from your plate, drink from your cup and sleep in your bed, I will dive into the pond and bring back your golden ball.'

'Yes, yes,' cried the princess unthinking, she was so eager to get her ball back. But to herself she thought, 'Who ever heard of a horrid frog living with a fair princess? Frogs are only for croaking in weedy ponds.' And she dismissed the thought with a shudder.

Yet the moment she had given her word, the frog had dived

deep into the pool. He soon reappeared with the ball in his mouth and dropped it at her feet.

The princess was overjoyed to see her pretty ball again. She quickly picked it up and ran off.

'Wait for me,' cried the frog. 'Take me with you. I cannot run as fast as you.'

But the princess did not give the frog a second thought. He could croak forever for all she cared, and in no time at all she forgot all about him.

Next day, just as the princess sat down to dinner with her sisters and father, a strange noise was heard coming up the marble staircase: pitter-patter-patter. Pitter-patter-patter. Then there came a gentle knock upon the door and a voice calling,

'Open the door, my honey, my dove.
Open the door to your own true love.'

The princess ran to the door and, flinging it open, was dismayed to see the frog outside. Banging the door shut again, she returned to her seat, her heart beating fast.

'My child, you look quite pale,' said the king. 'Who was that at the door?'

'A frog,' she said. 'A horrid frog.' And she told the story of her golden ball: how she had lost it in the water, promised the frog anything if he would fetch it, even saying he could live at the palace with her. She never dreamed he would keep her to her word.

As she was speaking, there came a knocking at the door again, toc-toc-toc, and the frog's voice called,

'Open the door, my honey, my dove.
Open the door to your own true love.'

'A promise is a promise,' said the king. 'Go and let him in.'

So the princess had to go and open the door to the visitor. In hopped the frog and he followed her to the table. As she sat down, he cried, 'Lift me up to sit beside you.'

The princess would have refused had the king not looked at her sternly.

When the frog was sitting beside her on the chair, he said, 'Now set me down beside your plate.' Then he said, 'Put your plate closer so that I can eat from it.'

Under her father's strict gaze, the princess did as the frog demanded, but not without a shiver of disgust. She could not bring herself to eat any more. Not so the frog. He ate to his heart's content.

'I'm full up now,' he said at last. 'And I'm tired after my long journey. Take me to your room, please, so that I can sleep beside you upon your pillow.'

That was too much for the princess. She burst into tears at the
thought of having a cold, clammy frog in her warm, clean bed.

But the king grew angry. 'When a princess gives her word,' he
said crossly, 'it must be kept. What you promised you must fulfil.'

So the princess picked up the frog between finger and thumb
and, holding him at arm's length, carried him up the stairs, much to
her sisters' amusement. Once inside her bedroom, she closed the
door and threw the frog into a corner before lying down in her bed to
sleep.

Just as her head touched the pillow, the frog called out, 'Put
me beside you on your pillow or I'll tell your father.'

There was nothing for it. She stepped out of bed, picked up the frog and set him down next to her on the silken pillow. He slept beside her the whole night through.

When the princess awoke next morning, she was astonished to find, not the frog, but a handsome prince standing beside her bed. He told her that a wicked witch had cast a spell on him and turned him into a frog. The spell would be lifted only when a princess could be found to let him sleep upon her bed.

'You, dear princess, broke the spell and I am free,' he said. 'Pray, be my wife and come with me to my father's kingdom.'

The young princess was not long in giving her consent, for to be sure he was a very handsome prince.

Next day, a coach drawn by eight white horses drew up at the palace gates. And there stood faithful Henry, the prince's servant. The poor man had grieved so hard for his master that his heart would surely have broken had he not bound it with three iron bands. He now seated the prince and princess in his coach, mounted up behind and off they drove to the prince's kingdom.

They had not gone far when there was an awful crack.

'Henry, the wheel has broken,' shouted the prince.

'No sire,' Henry replied. 'It is the band from round my heart.'

Twice more such cracks startled the prince. Yet, when he enquired about the coach's safety, Henry replied each time, 'No sire. It is only the band from round my heart.'

Faithful Henry was so overjoyed that his master was a frog no more, that the iron bands had broken.

THE EMPEROR'S NEW CLOTHES

A long time ago there lived an emperor who was so fond of clothes that he spent all his money on them. He had a new set of clothes for every hour of the day.

One day, two rascals came to town. They called themselves tailors, and said they could weave cloth of the most splendid pattern and colour; cloth that was invisible to anyone who was a fool.

'How wonderful,' thought the emperor. 'If I had clothes like that I would know which of my court was stupid. The cloth must be woven right away.' And he gave the two tailors a large sum of money to start work at once.

The two false tailors set up their looms and pretended to be busy though, truth to tell, they did nothing at all. They called for the most costly silk and pure gold thread, stuffed it into their bags and went on with their make-believe weaving deep into the night. All the townspeople heard of the wonderful cloth and were longing to learn how wise or stupid their neighbours were.

A few days passed, and the emperor wanted to know how his new clothes were coming along. He was, however, rather afraid, as he knew that a fool would not be able to see their beauty. Of course, he had nothing to worry about himself, but it might be wise to send someone else first.

'I know,' thought the emperor, 'I'll send my trusty old minister to see how things are progressing. He's the best to tell how it looks, for he is a man of good sense.'

So the old minister entered the chamber where the two rascals were pretending to work at the empty looms. He stared hard at the looms and said to himself, 'Well, that's extraordinary. I can't see a bit of thread on the frames.' But of course he did not speak his thoughts aloud.

The two rogues invited him closer and asked him if the style pleased him. Did he not think that the colours were beautiful? All the while, they pointed to the empty looms.

The poor minister looked as hard as he could, yet still saw nothing on the frames. 'I must be a fool,' he thought with shame. 'No one must know it.' So he peered closer at the loom, through his spectacles, and said out loud, 'Oh, it's simply delightful. What a pattern, what colours. Yes, I'll inform the emperor straight away.'

'We are so pleased you like it,' said the tailors, and they named all the patterns and colours they had used. The old minister listened closely so that he could repeat it all to the emperor.

Soon the whole city was talking about the magnificent cloth.

At last the emperor decided to see the precious cloth for himself while it was still upon the loom. Along with all the court nobles, he entered the chamber where the rascals were working away, pretending to make his suit of clothes.

'Isn't it beautiful?' said the old minister. 'Just look at the design and the colour.' And he pointed to the empty frames, believing that everybody else could see the fine workmanship.

'My goodness!' thought the emperor. 'I can't see a thing. Am I a fool and unfit to be ruler? Oh dear, Oh dear.' But out loud he said, 'Isn't it grand, isn't it great.'

All the while he nodded his head, smiling at everyone and staring closely at the empty looms. And the whole company now strained their eyes, hoping to see something fine upon the looms. But they saw no more than the emperor, and cried like him, 'Isn't it grand, isn't it great.'

They all advised him to have the cloth cut and sewn, so that he could wear the new suit in the coming parade. As for the two tailors, they were made Knights of the Garter and Tailors to the Emperor.

The night before the parade, that rascally pair sat up all night in the light of sixteen candles, so that all could see how keen they were to finish the emperor's new clothes. They pretended to roll the cloth from the looms. They cut the air with their scissors then sewed it with imaginary needles and thread. At long last they announced, 'The emperor's new clothes are ready.'

In the morning, the emperor went, together with his nobles, for the fitting. The tailors lifted their arms as if holding the cloth, saying, 'These are the trousers. This is the robe, this the cloak. It's as light as a cobweb. When it's on, sire, it'll feel like nothing at all. That is its charm, you see.'

'Yes, indeed,' breathed the nobles, though none of them saw a thing.

'If Your Majesty would just slip off his things,' said the men, 'we'll help him on with his new clothes. Over here by the mirror.'

The emperor willingly undressed, and the rascals pretended to dress him in his new clothes, turning him round so that he could see himself in the mirror from all sides.

Everybody admired the suit. 'How grand His Majesty looks.' 'What a perfect fit.' 'What colours.' 'What style.' Such were the cries all about, and the two lords of the bedchamber, who were to carry his cloak, bent down as if picking up the ends. They dared not admit they saw nothing.

Off went the emperor, walking in the parade through the streets of the city. And all the good people lining the streets or looking down from their windows gasped as they cried, 'Isn't it fine. Isn't it good. Isn't it absolutely grand.' No one dared admit that they could not see the suit. Never before had the emperor's clothes been such a success.

However, in the midst of all the claps and shouts, a child's voice was heard. 'But he's as naked as can be.'

There was an awful hush. Then the people began to pass on what the child had said, and at last a great shout went up:

'He really is as naked as can be.'

'The emperor's as naked as the day he was born.'

'He's in the altogether, his birthday suit.'

The emperor grew red with shame. He knew the people were right, but he had to end the parade in dignity. He walked on even more proudly, and the two gentlemen of the bedchamber took even greater pains to hold up the cloak that was not there.

Of course, the two tailors to the emperor had disappeared.

THE GOLDEN GOOSE

Once upon a time, there was a man and woman who had three sons. The two eldest were clever, the youngest was a fool. Everyone laughed at him and called him names.

One day, the eldest son was going to the forest to cut some logs. Before he went, his mother gave him a pork pie and a bottle of wine for his dinner. Off he went into the forest where he sat down to eat his meal.

No sooner had the boy taken out his food than a little old man appeared, bidding him good-day. 'Give us a bite to eat and a sip of wine,' the old man said. 'I'm so hungry and thirsty.'

But the clever young man replied, 'Give you a bite to eat and a sip of my wine? Certainly not. I haven't enough for myself, as it is.'

So the little old man wandered off.

When he had had his dinner the eldest son set to work, chopping down a tree: chip-chop-chop. But he had not been at it long before his axe slipped and caught him on the arm. At once he went home to have his arm bandaged.

The second son then went off to cut some logs, taking with him a pork pie and a bottle of wine. Once in the forest he was just sitting down to eat when that selfsame old man appeared, bidding him goodday. 'Give us a bite to eat and a sip of your wine,' he said.

But the lad was far too clever to be giving away his food. 'I've enough only for myself,' he said. 'Be off with you.'

Without a word the little old man wandered off.

The second son had only just set to cutting down the tree, chip-chop-chop, when his axe slipped and caught him a blow on the leg. So off home he limped.

Presently, the Fool said to his father, 'Father, let me go and cut some logs.'

But his father shook his head. 'No, no. Your brothers have both hurt themselves. You wouldn't know how to cut logs anyway. Stay at home.'

But the Fool kept on and on until, at last, his father gave in. 'Oh, all right. Perhaps you'll learn once you've chopped off an arm or a leg.'

The Fool's mother cared even less about him, and handed him a stale loaf and a bottle of sour beer. Off he marched into the forest, sat down on a tree stump and took out his food. Just as he was about to eat, the little old man appeared out of the trees, asking, 'Give us a bite to eat and a sip from your bottle. I'm so hungry and thirsty.'

'I've only dry bread and sour beer,' the Fool replied. 'But you're welcome to share them, if you wish.'

So they sat together, sharing the humble meal. Yet when the Fool took out his stale loaf he was surprised to find a freshly-baked cake; and when he took out his bottle of beer, he found it was now good wine.

When the meal was over, the old man said, 'Now I'm going to repay your kindness. Cut down that old tree over there and you'll see what you will see.' So saying, he vanished into thin air.

The Fool set to work: chip-chop-chop, chop-chip-chip, and he cut down the tree. What should he find in the hollow of its roots but a goose with feathers of pure gold. He picked it up and walked off with it under his arm.

The Fool had had enough of taunts at home, so he made up his mind to go into the world and seek his fortune. After a time, he came to an inn where he asked to spend the night. When he went upstairs to bed he left his goose upon a table in the bar.

Now the inn-keeper had three daughters, and the moment they set eyes upon the goose they all wanted a golden feather for themselves. As soon as the Fool had gone to bed, the eldest daughter crept over to the table and went to pull out a feather from the goose's wing. Yet as soon as she caught hold of it she could not pull her hand away. It was stuck fast.

As she was tugging and pulling, the second sister came along, intent on gaining a golden feather.

'My hand's stuck,' whispered the eldest girl. 'Pull me free.'

But as the second sister touched her arm she too stuck fast. Just then the third sister came up, and the other two cried out, 'We're stuck. Pull us off.'

But the moment the third sister took hold, she too stuck fast.

So the three sisters had to remain all night long stuck fast to the golden goose.

Next morning, the Fool came downstairs and had his breakfast, paying no attention to the three girls. When he was ready, he picked up his goose, put it under his arm and went off down the road.

Of course, like it or not, the three girls had to go with him. Wherever he went they were bound to follow, fast or slow, far or near. After a time he led them over a field and when they were half way across they met a vicar.

The good man wagged a finger at the three girls. 'Shame on you, running after this young man,' he scolded. And he went to take the youngest by the hand to pull her away. Yet the moment he touched her hand he too stuck fast and had to follow, willy-nilly, in her footsteps.

Not long after, as the five were going down a lane, the churchwarden came by. He stared in disbelief at the vicar chasing three young girls. 'Shame on you, vicar,' he cried. 'Have you

140

forgotten the christening today?' But when the vicar took no notice, the churchwarden ran after him and tugged his sleeve. He too stuck fast.

After a while, they passed two men hoeing potatoes.

'Help, help,' shouted the vicar. 'Pull us free.'

Of course, the moment the first man pulled at the churchwarden's belt he stuck fast; and as the other man pulled at him he stuck too. That made seven trotting behind the Fool and his goose.

Finally, they came to a big city. Now it so happened that the city was ruled by a king with an only daughter. Though beautiful,

the princess was a miserable soul. She never laughed and never smiled. So unhappy was the king that he had proclaimed: 'Whoever makes the princess laugh shall marry her.'

As soon as the Fool heard this, he led his strange procession to the palace, asking to be shown the sad princess. In went the Fool, pulling the innkeeper's three daughters, pulling the black-coated vicar, pulling the fat red churchwarden, pulling the men with their hoes, all treading on each other's heels and tripping over.

As soon as the princess saw this funny sight, her sad face broke into a smile. Then she laughed and laughed and laughed until the tears ran down her cheeks.

That broke the spell. The goose gave a hiss. The seven followers fell back in a heap, and the Fool claimed his bride.

In time, he became king, and he ruled no less wisely than those who had gone before.